The
CLOCKWORK
QUEEN

PETER BUNZL

Illustrated by
LIA VISIRIN

To Georgia

First published in 2022 in Great Britain by
Barrington Stoke Ltd
18 Walker Street, Edinburgh, EH3 7LP

www.barringtonstoke.co.uk

Text © 2022 Peter Bunzl
Illustrations © 2022 Lia Visirin

A CIP catalogue record for this book is available
from the British Library upon request

ISBN: 978-1-80090-080-6

Printed by Hussar Books, Poland

CONTENTS

Mama   Papa   Sophie

Olga   Mr Kon   Prince
Paul   Empress
Catherine

1

AN OPENING MOVE

The weather in Moscow was beautiful on my tenth birthday. Cherry blossoms fell from the trees in the park. The sun dazzled off the dome of St Basil's Cathedral. The air was filled with joy and laughter. It felt as if the whole world was happy.

The whole world except me.

I was filled with sadness as my beloved papa was leaving us. Papa had put on his wig, and Mama had ironed his smartest shirt and cleaned his best coat. He held his leather satchel filled with his books, papers, chess board and chess pieces under his arm.

Papa was an expert chess player – the best in Russia. Empress Catherine the Great was a famous chess player too. Papa was going away because she had asked him to come to St Petersburg to teach her son Paul to play.

Prince Paul was ten. The same age as me. I was surprised that he didn't know chess already. Papa had been teaching me since I was five. Perhaps princes had other things to do?

It was a great honour for Papa to be invited to the Winter Palace in St Petersburg, but Mama and I didn't know how long he would be away. He had promised to write to us and send money so we would be looked after. But how would we cope without him?

Papa held my hand and Mama's as the three of us walked across the park towards the coach station. A porter followed a few steps behind us, pushing Papa's luggage on a trolley.

We passed the fountain and the square with its rows of rusty tables. This was where Papa and I often went to play chess with others.

The people who played chess there wore old clothes, but they had sharp minds. They gathered every day to challenge each other to lively games. Our family knew them well. The chess players waved to Papa and Mama and me as we passed.

"Hello, Ivan Peshka!" one shouted.

"Hello, Anya Peshka!" another called out.

"Hello, little Sophie!" said a third player.

"Hello, Mr Ferz, Miss Petrov, Miss Damka, Mr Slon," I called back.

"Come and play!" they said.

"Can we?" I asked Papa and Mama.

"Not today," said Mama, and shook her head.

"I am on my way to St Petersburg!" Papa told everyone.

"Good luck!" they shouted.

I slowed to try to watch the games, but there wasn't time to chat. Papa and Mama were in a hurry to reach the coach station.

*

The coach station was busy, filled with horses, trolleys and porters with trunks. Travellers lined up to board stagecoaches and carriages. Street sellers with handcarts sold steaming pies. Papa's coach was delayed for at least an hour, so we found seats in a waiting room.

"Is there time for Sophie and me to have a game?" Papa asked Mama, who was looking at the big clock in the station. "It's our last chance before I leave."

"One quick one," Mama sighed, and blew her nose. Her eyes were full of tears, but she tried not to show it. "I'll go and see what has happened to your trunk."

"Thank you, dear." Papa kissed Mama and gave her some coins to pay the porter.

Mama hurried back across the coach station, and Papa and I set up his chess board to play.

The people in the waiting room began to talk behind their hands. "Look," one of them whispered. "It's the famous chess player Ivan Peshka and his daughter."

Soon a crowd had gathered to watch us. I wasn't nervous. I was a bit of a show-off really, and I normally liked playing in front of crowds. But not today – today I wanted Papa all to myself. It had been a long time since we had played a game alone. Even our first game was in public. I thought back to it now.

It had been in the same park we'd just walked across. I was only five. The sun was shining like today. Papa and Mama and I were walking around and eating ices.

We stopped at the tables in the square to watch the games. When the players saw Papa, they all wanted to play him. But Papa said no – it was his day off with his family.

Then Papa saw I was fiddling with the chess pieces beside one of the boards. I was trying to copy the way the players moved them. That was the day he decided he would teach me chess.

Papa got out his board and we found a free table and started right there. That was how I had my first lesson, with Mama watching and the regular chess players looking on.

Papa and I played many games of chess over the years – in the park and at home after supper with Mama. Papa taught me everything he knew, and I got better and better. But I didn't know it was leading up to today and our last game together in the coach station.

I couldn't focus on our game. There was too much noise. Too much on my mind. I played as best I could, making instinctive moves. I paused and looked up, realising that Papa had captured most of my pieces.

"Focus, Sophie," he said. "Remember what I told you: the most important thing is to have a good opening strategy and a strong endgame."

Finally, Papa trapped my king in a corner of the board and made his winning move.

Checkmate.

He tipped my king over to show I had lost.

The other travellers in the waiting room clapped politely.

"I'm sorry," I cried. I brushed my sleeve across my face to hold back the sadness. I felt devastated. Not to lose the game but because Papa was going away. "I don't want you to leave."

"I have to," Papa replied softly as he packed away the chess pieces.

"What if you don't come back?" I said. "St Petersburg is a long way."

Papa laughed. "Then you can come and find me."

"Really?" I asked.

"No." Papa shook his head. "Not really. You must stay here with Mama."

"Oh," I said sadly.

I looked up to see Mama dashing across the station.

"You'd best get a move on!" Mama called as she burst through the door. "Your carriage is here and waiting to depart!"

"Of course, dear," Papa said. He stood and kissed her.

"Please don't go," I said. "Let's play again."

"It's not for ever, Sophie." Papa ruffled my hair. "I'll be back before you know it. In the meantime, here's a going-away present." He took something from his bag – a package wrapped in string and brown paper.

I tore it open. It was Papa's book, *Masters of Chess*.

I flipped through the pages, which contained drawings and descriptions of the world's most famous chess players and games.

"Practise with my pieces," Papa said, placing his board and box into my arms. "Learn from the masters in this book. Then, the next time we meet, you will be good enough to beat me."

"ALL ABOARD THE COACH FOR ST PETERSBURG!" the station master called.

"Hurry," Mama muttered tearfully.

Papa gave us both one final hug goodbye and dashed out of the waiting room.

Mama and I watched through the window as Papa climbed aboard his coach.

Papa leaned from the window and waved at us as the coach pulled out of the yard. Then he was gone.

2

THE RULES OF THE GAME

The first time Papa and I played chess, I took in all the pieces as Papa tipped them from the box. Their different shapes and sizes reminded me of toy soldiers.

"The chess board has sixty-four squares," Papa explained as he laid the pieces out. "Thirty-two black squares and thirty-two white ones. There are two players and each has sixteen pieces. Each piece is important in the game."

Papa arranged the pieces into two black rows in front of me and two white rows in front

of him. There were eight pieces in each row.
"There," he said when he was finished. "Now
we're ready to begin."

"Where's the dice?" I asked.

Papa laughed. "Chess doesn't have dice,
Sophie. It's a battle of wits."

I gripped the smallest piece in my tiny hand.
It was a round ball set on a circular column.

"That's a pawn," Papa said. "A brave little
soldier. It may not be mighty, but it has
courage. There's a big reward for a pawn
who reaches the far side of the board – it's
crowned queen."

My heart soared. To start out a pawn and
become a queen was an exciting thought.

Papa reached for a piece with a crown on its
head and held it up.

"The queen is the strongest piece on the board," he explained. "She's clever enough to outwit her enemies, like our Empress Catherine. Did you know Empress Catherine was called Sophie when she was young?"

"Like me!" I said.

Papa nodded. "We named you after her. Sophie was brought to Russia by her mother and told she had to marry her second cousin, Prince Peter, whom she didn't really like. But the marriage went ahead, and Sophie became a princess. She even changed her name to Catherine in honour of Peter's grandmother.

"Princess Catherine made friends over the years and became wise in the ways of the Russian Court. When the old Empress, Elizabeth, died, Peter became the new Emperor with Catherine at his side. But Peter was a bad ruler, so Catherine decided to fight him for the crown. Catherine and her friends made a cunning plan. They fought Peter and won. Then Catherine became the Empress and ruler of Russia."

"Is that the aim of chess?" I asked. "To defeat your enemy?"

"Yes," Papa said. "Especially their king."

He picked up another piece with a crown and held it up beside the queen.

"The king is weak, as powerful men sometimes are. He relies on his army for protection. But with skill and cunning, you can defeat him. Just as the great Empress Catherine defeated Peter to become our Queen."

Papa put his king and queen back on the board and showed me the rest of the pieces.

There were two horses, two figures in helmets and two towers.

"Knights, bishops and castles," Papa explained.

I listened as he told me how each piece moved and fought. The castles went in straight lines. The bishops diagonally. The knights moved in an L-shape, like leaping horses. When he'd finished, Papa said, "Shall we play?"

I nodded eagerly. My head was spinning with everything I'd learned as we began.

Papa moved his king's pawn first.

I copied his move with my own king's pawn, and the game started.

Then Papa moved his king's knight, and I moved mine.

As we played on, Papa showed me how to take pieces. He helped me take one of his pawns with a side-step move called *en passant*.

A few turns later, Papa took one of my knights and explained how he had planned ahead many moves ago to do just that.

Gradually, I was drawn in to the game. It felt like I was sending wooden warriors into battle. I never wanted it to end.

Except it did. Five years later, on the day I turned ten. When Papa left for St Petersburg, and Mama and I found ourselves alone.

*

After Papa left, I went to the park beside
St Basil's Cathedral to practise chess every day.
Papa used to take me, but now I went alone.
I used his board and box of hand-carved pieces
to challenge the regular players.

Every night at home, I read Papa's book.
Then, after dinner, Mama and I wrote to Papa.
I told him about playing chess in the park. I
drew the board and noted the moves so Papa
could see the sequences I had played.

At first, Papa wrote back to us often. He sent
bank notes from the treasury of the Empress
and long letters that Mama and I loved reading.

The first few pages were always filled with
tales of the glamorous life at the palace. The
next few contained stories of Papa's struggles to
teach the young prince to play chess. He said
Paul was a terrible player, with no patience,
discipline, interest or will to learn. Paul was

stubborn in his refusal to improve under Papa's guidance, despite the Empress's wishes.

But the months went by, and the letters and money started to arrive less and less frequently. Finally, they stopped altogether.

The last package we received from the palace was not from Papa but from the office of the Empress. We knew this because it was stamped with her seal. The envelope contained a pile of our unopened letters and a short message signed by Mr Ladya, the Empress's personal secretary.

From the Office of Empress Catherine.

Ivan Peshka is no longer receiving mail. He has been imprisoned in the dungeons of the Winter Palace by order of the Empress for his failure to teach her son to play chess.

My heart dropped to my boots. Mama's face turned the colour of raw dumplings. She screwed the letter into a ball and threw it across the room.

"The Empress is a cruel woman," Mama said. "She has done many good things for this country, but she has too much power. Your papa has done nothing wrong."

"What should we do?" I asked.

Mama thought for a moment. "We must put right this terrible wrong. We will raise funds for someone to go to the palace and request that the Empress release Papa."

The next day, Mama wrote to a lawyer in St Petersburg to ask for his help. Mama sent the last of our savings with the letter. The lawyer took the money but never replied. We could do no more.

*

A year had passed, along with my eleventh
birthday. Mama and I lived off the small
payments for Papa's book that arrived from
booksellers.

Eventually, even those ran out. We had to
sell what possessions we had, but I insisted we
keep Papa's book and chess set. Those gifts
were all I had left of him, and I refused to let
them go.

The sale of our things raised just enough
money for us to move into new lodgings.
It was a small, cramped single room on
Shakhmaty Street. For a while, Mama worked
as a seamstress sewing pieces of fabric, and
I helped her. But then that job finished, and
there was nothing more.

That winter was the coldest in years. One
night Mama fell terribly ill with a fever and took

to her bed. A week later she went to sleep and never woke up.

At the age of eleven, I was alone in the world. I had a handful of coins – barely enough to buy food – and Papa's book and chess set.

I wrote to Papa telling him the awful news, hoping that somehow the letter would reach him. I addressed it to his quarters in the Winter Palace, but it was returned to me unopened.

It felt horrific to me that Papa didn't know of Mama's passing or the difficult situation I now found myself in.

The chess players in the park took pity on me and helped me out as much as they could. They taught me their best moves and set me up to play games with strangers to win money.

I became a champion player – with their help and the knowledge I had gained from reading Papa's book. I could beat any opponent. I won just enough money to live. It wasn't much of a life, but I was able to scrape by. At least until I made other plans.

I was determined that one day I would earn enough money for the fare to St Petersburg. Then I would go to the Winter Palace and request that the Empress release Papa. If she refused, I would find a way to rescue him.

It was barely a plan, and I would not be able to achieve it alone. I had no savings and St Petersburg was hundreds of miles away. I knew I needed as much help as I could get.

Then one day out of the blue, that help arrived in the shape of Miss Olga Kon.

3

PELMENI FOR DINNER

It was a dusky evening at the end of winter.
Over two years had passed since Papa and I
played our last game of chess together in the
Moscow coach station. It had been thirteen
months since Papa had been imprisoned.
Eleven months since Mama's tragic death.

I was twelve. I still played chess in the park
every day, but life was hard. I had beaten all
the players and the visitors many times. They
were fed up with me winning. They had stopped
paying to play against me or to watch me play.

I had no money left. In a week's time, I
would be thrown out of my lodgings. With a

heavy heart I realised that tomorrow I would have to try to sell Papa's chess set.

The park players were packing up for the night. I was putting Papa's chess pieces away for the last time when I glanced up to see a girl in a black dress waving at everyone.

25

"Hello, Mr Ferz, Miss Petrov, Miss Damka, Mr Slon," the girl called.

The regulars waved back and called hello. They seemed to know her, and I realised I recognised her too. Her name was Olga Kon. She was a few years older than me and a few inches taller.

Olga's father was an inventor who made clockwork machines. Mr Kon and Papa had been friends. Mr Kon was a good chess player. I had played against him many times in the old days. Olga too. She and he used to come to the park to play chess a lot. Then, one day, they had stopped.

Papa told me that Mr Kon and Olga had moved to the city of Smolensk, where workshop space was cheaper. We never found out what Mr Kon was working on there. But now Olga had returned after five years.

"Hello, Sophie," Olga said. She stepped across the square to my table. "Perhaps you don't recognise me? We played many times in the past."

"I remember, Olga," I replied.

"I've been watching your games this past week," Olga said.

"I haven't seen you," I said.

"That is because I didn't want to be seen," Olga said. "Not until now."

She was tall and grown up, and I felt very intimidated standing opposite her.

"We heard about your father," Olga went on. She looked around to make sure no one was listening. "He's imprisoned at the Winter Palace."

What was it to her? I ignored her remark.
I'd almost finished packing away anyway.

One chess piece was missing. I searched but
couldn't find it.

"Where is she?" I muttered.

"Looking for this?" Olga said, and handed
me the white queen. "I saw you playing Mr Ferz
yesterday. He knows every opening gambit.
And Miss Damka before that. She has a good
line in endgames. And Miss Petrov. She always
castles early. And Mr Slon, who likes to play
the Queen's Gambit. You beat them all, Sophie.
You are a great player. Easily as good as your
father."

"Not for much longer," I said. "I can't go on
like this. Tomorrow I must sell Papa's chess set
and make a new start. Now what is it you want,
Olga?" I added angrily. I felt tired and ready to
go back to my lodgings.

"I want to challenge you to one last game," Olga said.

I shook my head.

"Not against me," Olga added hurriedly. "Against a professional player."

"I told you, I cannot," I said. "I need to get home. Mama will be waiting."

"I know that's not true." Olga stared at my worn clothes, my cold gloveless hands and my sad lonely eyes. "Your mother is gone. You are all alone in the world. Let me take you to play one match. My father will be there. He will pay you well whether you win or lose."

"Where is this game?" I asked.

"Nearby," Olga said. "Not very far. On the way I will buy you dinner. Whatever you like."

"Pelmeni," I said. "I like pelmeni dumplings with sour cream. If you get me those, and the money, then I will play chess against any opponent you choose."

"Pelmeni it is." Olga smiled and took my arm. "I know a good restaurant called Korol's where we can eat like kings."

*

The tablecloths in Korol's were starched bright white and the silver cutlery sparkled in the candlelight. The walls were covered in velvet and crowded with gold-framed paintings. The waiter pulled out a chair for Olga and then one for me as we sat down.

Olga ordered two portions of pelmeni.

"This is where Papa and I like to eat when we are visiting Moscow," she explained.

"Where is your papa?" I asked, looking around for him.

"He is preparing for the game tonight," Olga said. "So dinner will be only you and me. But not to worry, you will meet Papa later at the chess match."

"Do you often visit smart places like this in Moscow? Or in other cities?" I asked. Olga and her father must have been doing well. Her life seemed very glamorous. I guessed it must have something to do with chess, or perhaps the mechanical work her father did. I wasn't sure yet what that work was.

"What do you Kons do?" I asked.

Olga flicked out her napkin and placed it daintily on her lap. "We put on show games of chess in the homes of rich and famous people. Sometimes for dukes and duchesses; sometimes for kings and queens. We are going to St Petersburg very soon. Have you been?"

I shook my head. Olga smiled. She seemed to know what I was going to say before I did. She was always thinking ahead, ever the chess player.

"If you win the game tonight, we will take you to St Petersburg," she said. "We will pay your way. We might even be able to help you with the problem with your papa."

My heart leapt. That was a prize worth aiming for. I needed to win this coming match.

The pelmeni arrived. They were so steaming hot that I almost burned the roof of my mouth as I bit into one. Still, they were the best I'd tasted.

"Who am I playing tonight?" I asked while I waved a hand in front of my face to reduce the heat of the dumplings.

"The Clockwork Queen," Olga replied, and leaned across the table. "Have you heard of her?"

I shook my head. It was a strange nickname, but many players used them, especially the successful ones. Maybe this player had a mind as sharp as clockwork?

"Is she famous?" I asked.

"She's the greatest player in all of Russia," Olga said. "She has a mind like a steel engine. But I bet you can beat her."

"Really?" I asked, unsure. I wondered if Olga was right.

"Really," Olga said. "The Clockwork Queen is playing tonight at the Moscow Chess Club."

I had heard of the Moscow Chess Club from Papa and the players in the park. It was a famous institution. To think I would have the chance to play against the Clockwork Queen there, whoever she was. I felt a bit scared at that prospect, but I couldn't refuse Olga's invitation. I needed the money she had offered, as well as her help to get to St Petersburg and to find Papa.

4

THE MOSCOW CHESS CLUB

"Welcome to the Moscow Chess Club!" Olga said
as she pushed open a door with a brass knocker
in the shape of a pawn. I stared up at the
building's grand entrance with its tall columns.
I felt a twinge of doubt as I followed Olga inside.

We went past a smart ticket seller in a
small lobby and stepped into a room not unlike
a large theatre, but without seats. It was filled
with elegantly dressed people – men in long
coats and women in fashionable dresses, their
hair decorated with ribbons and feathers.

I stood on my tiptoes and craned my neck to
see between the heads of the crowd.

Everyone had arranged themselves in a loose circle around a low stage. In the centre of the stage was a large object hidden beneath a plain woven cloth.

"What's under there?" I asked Olga.

"The Clockwork Queen," Olga replied.

I shook my head. I didn't believe it. Why would a chess champion be sitting in the middle of a room with a cloth over her head? I knew from Papa's book that the greatest chess players could be strange, but I had never heard of one with such an odd habit.

Just as I was thinking this, a man appeared from backstage – Mr Kon. He bowed so deeply to the audience that I saw his bald patch hidden below the black swirl of his hair. His bright eyes took in the room, as quick as a fox, then paused on me and darted to Olga.

"Thank you for coming," Mr Kon said with a smile. He was more of a showman than I remembered. I looked around for Olga to tell her this, but she had disappeared.

"I am Mr Kon," he went on. "Chess fan, master mechanic and creator and owner of the Clockwork Queen. Nervous quests may want to wait in the lobby as she can be *quite* unsettling."

No one left.

"As you wish," Mr Kon said. "Ladies and gentlemen, may I present Her Mechanical Majesty!"

Mr Kon pulled away the cover. I stared, shocked at the figure and cabinet beneath it. So this was what Mr Kon had been busy creating in his workshop in Smolensk all these years.

The Clockwork Queen wore a cloak trimmed with fur and a tin crown decorated with glass beads. Her wooden body was jointed with metal hinges, and an iron key poked out from her side. Her hair was polished brown and her face was painted brightly, with blushed cheeks and a straight nose. I could see woodgrain under old patches of her paintwork.

Mr Kon set a large chess board down on the cabinet between the Queen's wooden hands. The oak cabinet was about the size of a chest of drawers. Then he took out some beautifully carved chess pieces and arranged them on the board in front of the Clockwork Queen.

Lastly, Mr Kon stepped to one side and opened two doors in the cabinet to reveal what was inside. The cabinet was filled with cogs and springs, all connected together. It looked like the complex machinery of a giant music box.

Mr Kon slowly turned the key on the Clockwork Queen's side in a clockwise direction. The machinery in the cabinet began to move and a ticking noise started up.

"These are the wheels and gears that move the Clockwork Queen's mind and body," Mr Kon explained.

I had barely taken in the Queen's intricate interior before Mr Kon finished winding her and closed the doors of the cabinet.

"You have witnessed the workings of the device," he said. "So now let us examine our player."

He moved the Queen's cloak aside, revealing a hatch hidden in her chest. I hoped the Queen's body didn't contain any human organs. That would be too strange. But Mr Kon opened this hatch and all I saw was a selection of more cogs, plus brass tubes and pulleys that ran through the centre of the Queen's body.

Mr Kon closed the hatch and returned to the front of the stage. There was a loud *CRUNCH*, and the Clockwork Queen turned her head jerkily, taking in the whole crowd. The audience burst into applause.

"Do not look the Queen directly in the eye," Mr Kon warned. "She can see into your soul."

The applause stopped, and everyone looked away.

The Clockwork Queen sat up straighter, and her eyes fell on me.

I shifted uncomfortably.

The Clockwork Queen nodded with approval. Then she lowered her head to examine the board.

"The Queen always moves first," Mr Kon said, and put a hand lightly on her arm. "We allow her that advantage as she is made of clockwork!" He smiled at the crowd. "I am afraid we will only have time for one challenger tonight. A guest player has been invited specially to the Moscow Chess Club for the occasion. Please welcome Miss Peshka!"

My stomach dropped. Olga must have told her father she had managed to persuade me to play. But I hadn't realised I would be the only one. I looked around again for Olga, but she had left me alone.

Now that I had seen the Clockwork Queen, I no longer felt so sure about playing her. She looked scary. No one in the crowd knew who I was – perhaps I could still sneak away? I ducked my head and took a step back, but Mr Kon had spotted me.

"There she is!" he called out. "MISS PESHKA!"

Everyone turned and stared. I scanned their faces, looking for Olga, but I could not see her.

"Come along, Sophie!" Mr Kon called. "Her Mechanical Majesty awaits!"

The crowd parted, making a path to the stage. Olga had promised that if I won, she and her father would take me to St Petersburg. Where was Olga? It seemed vital she saw the match, and she still had not returned. I wondered what Papa would do in my position, and in that moment I decided to play.

5

THE CLOCKWORK QUEEN

Nerves fluttered in my stomach as I stepped through the crowd, preparing myself to face the Clockwork Queen. Mr Kon told everyone about me as I walked towards the stage.

"Sophie is twelve. She plays chess in the park. You might think she's hardly a suitable opponent for the Clockwork Queen. But Sophie's father is the famous grandmaster Ivan Peshka. He wrote the book on chess."

Mr Kon whipped out a copy of Papa's book from behind his back and waved it in the air. A moment later, the book was gone. Like a magician, he'd made it disappear.

"Ivan Peshka taught Sophie everything he knew," Mr Kon said. "Tonight, she will be the youngest player ever to challenge the Clockwork Queen. Perhaps she's nervous? Maybe she fears letting her father down? Sophie needs encouragement. Please give her a round of applause as she joins me."

The crowd clapped as I climbed up onto the stage and sat down opposite the Clockwork Queen.

"If checkmate occurs, the Clockwork Queen will indicate this with three nods," Mr Kon explained to everyone. "If the game is not finished after an hour, whoever is in the strongest position will be declared the winner."

He leaned forward and whispered in my ear, "Be sure not to cheat, Sophie. The Clockwork Queen will know, and your turn will be over."

Then Mr Kon went and sat down on a chair at the far side of the stage.

His advice made me even more nervous.

I tried to tell myself the Clockwork Queen was no different to the opponents I had faced in the past. But that wasn't true. She *was* different. She was a complex machine designed to learn and play against the best players in the world. How could I beat her?

I would have to try if I wanted to go with Olga and Mr Kon to St Petersburg and find Papa. I was still thinking this when the Clockwork Queen raised her arm with a creak. She opened her clawed fingers, grasped one of her pawns and moved it two squares forward.

I responded by moving one of my pawns.

The game had begun.

*

Every time the Clockwork Queen took one of my pieces, she grasped it and placed it beside her.

Then she moved her attacking piece into the empty square.

I tapped my fingers nervously on the cabinet. Gradually, I was beginning to work out what kind of player the Clockwork Queen was. Her movements were slow and deliberate, unlike the speed players in the park. She considered each move carefully, watching me before she committed.

Her blank face made me anxious. I could read nothing from it. I felt as if her glass eyes could really see me. I remembered what Mr Kon had said about her seeing into your soul and tried not to return her gaze.

The Clockwork Queen played with the clarity of a master. I knew that complex thinking was going on somewhere inside her mechanical mind. And that scared me most of all.

Chess to me was all about instincts. Heart choices and head choices. The Clockwork Queen had neither of those. She was all cogs and wheels inside. *How can she play chess like a human? Where do her thoughts and strategies come from? Is someone helping her?*

These questions began to distract me from the game.

I glanced at Mr Kon, who was leaning forward in his seat. He was watching my moves like a hawk.

He didn't seem to be controlling the Clockwork Queen. Neither did anyone in the audience. They were too far away. It had to be something else.

I began making bold moves to try to throw the Clockwork Queen off.

Each time I sat back and watched how she reacted.

But the Queen was a strong player. She took control of the board early.

Mid-game I was able to mount a fight back and captured both her knights. But the Clockwork Queen recovered quickly. By the

endgame she had taken my queen. To finish, she checkmated me with a surprising sequence of moves I had not seen coming.

Then the Clockwork Queen gave three sharp nods to show that she'd won.

I clenched my fists and stared angrily at her. Her wooden face seemed unbearably smug. I wondered if I should tell her that she'd ruined my life. But then I realised she was only a machine. She couldn't understand and she wouldn't care.

"Thank you for watching, ladies and gentlemen," Mr Kon said at the end of the game. "I think you will agree that was a breath-taking match. Please give a round of applause to young Sophie!"

The crowd clapped politely, but I ignored them. I stood up from the board, distraught. Olga had promised I could come to St Petersburg with her if I won the match, but I hadn't. I had

lost. And badly. There was no chance she and
her father would take me there now.

"You played very well," Mr Kon said, giving
me a pat on the back. "For a moment, I thought
you were going to beat us."

He glanced at the Clockwork Queen Now
the game was over, her mechanisms had wound
down. She was frozen as still as a statue. Her
unmoving face looked prim and unfeeling. I
hated her. That stupid machine.

"Honoured guests!" Mr Kon called to the
audience. "The show is over. There will be no
more play tonight!"

The audience stamped their feet restlessly
and sighed.

Mr Kon raised a hand to quieten them.
"I'm afraid our time is up this evening. But
I promise, when the Clockwork Queen next
returns to Moscow, the chess club will be the

first to know. There will be announcements in the press – and more games!"

He threw the cloth cover back over the Clockwork Queen.

I wanted to ask Mr Kon about my payment, but he strode off the stage to attend to some business outside.

The crowd began to file out of the back doors. I looked around for Olga, but she was still missing. A part of me was glad she hadn't witnessed my defeat. Olga had seemed sure I would win. I wondered why she had chosen to leave without watching the game.

Suddenly, a hand tapped me on the arm. I turned to find a grinning Olga standing beside me. She had appeared from nowhere. It was like being blindsided by a magic trick, or an unexpected chess move.

"That was a very close match," Olga said. "You almost won." She didn't look disappointed. In fact, she looked excited.

"What do you mean?" I asked angrily. "You missed the whole game."

"Oh no, I saw it." Olga laughed. "You just didn't see me. I had a special seat—"

"Don't lie," I interrupted. "You left me in this strange place to face the Clockwork Queen alone. I lost, and everyone was disappointed. Your father's gone. He hasn't paid me, and I won't be able to come to St Petersburg!" I burst into tears.

"Don't cry, Sophie." Olga's eyes twinkled in the candlelight. "The game's not over. In fact, it's only just begun. Come on." She put her arm through mine. "I'll show you the real reason I brought you here tonight."

Then Olga led me back to the centre of the stage, where the Clockwork Queen was hidden beneath her cover.

6

THE SECRET COMPARTMENT

I was still snivelling as Olga pulled the cover off the Clockwork Queen. Just then her father reappeared at the back of the room, clutching a wad of money.

"There she is!" Mr Kon cried. "Little Sophie Peshka, daughter of the world's greatest chess master. Legend of the park! Champion in waiting! And my Olga, who found her again."

He leapt onto the stage and went on, "I must say, you put on quite the show, Miss Peshka. You almost had the Clockwork Queen beat. This isn't only the ticket takings." He waved his wad of cash. "Many of the members of the famous

Moscow Chess Club bet against us during the game. Thanks to you, we made a decent haul!"

I didn't know what to say. So I didn't say anything. I just waited for him to continue.

"You're what we're looking for, Sophie." Mr Kon smiled at me, then turned to his daughter. "She will be a worthy replacement for you, Olga, in the St Petersburg match."

I had no idea what he was talking about. "What do you mean, 'a worthy replacement'?" I asked. "I thought you said you would only take me to St Petersburg if I won?"

"You may not have won," Olga said. "But you were very close. You're the most original player we know, Sophie."

"Not to mention the smallest," Mr Kon added. "That's important too."

I brushed a hand across my face to dry my tears. "Who will I be playing against?" I asked.

"Catherine the Great! Empress of all Russia!" Mr Kon said.

I gasped. "That's why you're taking me to St Petersburg?" I asked, flabbergasted. "You want me to play chess against the Empress in the Winter Palace?"

"Father was certain you were the one to play Empress Catherine," Olga said. "And I thought he was right after I saw you playing again in the park. But I had to be sure. So I brought you here to test your skills against the Clockwork Queen."

"I don't understand," I said. "I know I probably shouldn't say this, because I need your help to get to St Petersburg, but the Clockwork Queen is a much better player than me. You should take *her* to play against the Empress."

Mr Kon laughed. "Oh, Sophie!" he said. "The Clockwork Queen *will* be playing the Empress. And *you* will be playing for her!"

"And in return," Olga said, "we will sneak you into the Winter Palace so you can try to find your father."

"Your father was a good friend to me when Olga and I lived in Moscow," Mr Kon said. "I read about his imprisonment and heard about your poor mother. I thought we might be able to help each other now you are on your own."

This was all too confusing. "But how will we help each other?" I asked. "How will I play for the Clockwork Queen?"

"Perhaps this will clear things up," Mr Kon said.

He and Olga took me round to the back of the Clockwork Queen and Mr Kon pulled the blanket aside. Olga knelt down by the Queen's

feet and pressed a knot of wood on the rear
panel of the cabinet.

WHOOSH! The panel slid open, revealing a
secret compartment a child could comfortably
squeeze into.

That was it, I realised. Olga had been in there! That was where she had disappeared to during the game. She had been playing the Clockwork Queen!

Olga smiled when she saw I had worked it out.

"I direct the Clockwork Queen," she said. "From this secret compartment, hidden inside the box."

"So all those cogs and wheels are fake?" I asked. "And the Queen can't play chess herself? It's a trick?"

"That's right." Olga nodded. "I've been playing for her since she was first built."

"I spent years trying to design a real machine that could play chess as well as the greatest chess players," Mr Kon said. "But I was never able to do it. Then I realised I had already made a chess prodigy who could puppeteer the machine for me and make it look real – Olga."

"But why not just play chess as yourself?" I asked Olga.

"You know why," she replied. "Society makes it harder for us girls to play professionally. That's one reason. The other is that everyone's seen human players before. But a Clockwork Queen – that's impossible! Who wouldn't pay to see that?"

Olga shook her head. "But I'm getting too old to play for the Clockwork Queen now. I'm almost too tall to fit in the secret compartment. So we needed to find someone new."

"That is where you come in," Mr Kon said. "I promised Olga that if she could get me a player good enough and small enough to replace her, she could run the show with me."

"I wouldn't have to climb into that tiny cabinet and hide myself away any more," Olga said. "And I wouldn't have to spend my entire life with a brain full of chess puzzles. That's why I brought you here tonight, Sophie. To offer you this job. The role of the Clockwork Queen."

I thought about it.

Did I want to climb into that machine? Hide inside that uncomfortable secret compartment in the cabinet? If I said yes, I would be going with the Kons to St Petersburg and the Winter Palace, where Papa was imprisoned. All I'd have to do was agree to play as the Clockwork Queen against the Empress. After the game, surely I could find a chance to speak to the Empress and beg her to free Papa?

Papa had always told me a clever pawn could become a queen. That had seemed an impossible goal for me at the time. But now here were the Kons offering me that chance.

I looked at their expectant faces. And at the unmoving mask of the Clockwork Queen.

She was a piece on the chess board. No more. No less.

She was a role I would need to play to get Papa back.

I couldn't refuse such an offer.

My stomach fluttered nervously as I bent down and peered into the gap to the secret compartment in the cabinet beneath the Clockwork Queen.

"All right," I agreed. "I'll do it."

7

PRACTICE MAKES PERFECT

The inside of the Clockwork Queen's cabinet was dark and cramped. I had to bend my body into an L-shape in order to fit around all the levers and pulleys. The jagged controls stuck into me at all angles. I shifted, trying to make myself comfortable.

Olga passed me a lit candle. "Put this candle there," she insisted, pointing at a shelf in the corner. "There are a few secret holes hidden in the cabinet to let the air in, but they don't provide much light, so you still need the candle to see."

Olga shut the secret door, trapping me inside the cabinet.

I was scared at first. I'd never been anywhere so claustrophobic. My back ached from the weird position I was squashed into. The air inside was hot and dusty. It felt like I was a shirt folded in a chest of drawers. I began scrabbling around, as scared as a rat caught in a trap.

"Be calm," said Olga. "Take deep breaths. It can take a while to get used to the space."

I took deep breaths as she advised. After a while, my panic began to fade and I got used to being inside the small cabinet.

I looked around in the dim candlelight. By my right arm were three metal levers with various brakes and wires attached to them.

The wires ran up from the levers into the Clockwork Queen's body above.

"What do these levers do?" I called to Olga and Mr Kon.

I wasn't sure if my voice would be muffled by the wood, but Mr Kon seemed to hear me just fine.

"The middle lever controls the Queen's head," he said. "The left one controls her left arm and the right one controls her right arm."

"Give it a go," Olga said. "Get used to it."

"All right."

I took hold of the central lever and the left one and began to move them slowly. I heard the Queen move creakily outside. There was a periscope that ran up to the Clockwork Queen's head. I peered into its viewer and saw out through the Queen's glass eyes. I could see the whole of the chess board and the room beyond it.

"Ready?" Olga asked. She sat down on the opposite side of the board and looked the Queen straight in the eyes.

I could see her quite clearly through the periscope. I pulled the middle lever and made the Clockwork Queen nod. Then I gripped the right lever. With gentle control, I was able to get the Queen to grasp one of her pawns and make the first move.

Olga moved a black pawn, and the game began.

*

We practised late into the night. I knew I had to be good for Mr Kon and Olga to agree to take me to St Petersburg.

Olga gave me as much advice on controlling the Clockwork Queen as she could. The longer the game continued, the better I got at working the levers and dials inside the secret compartment.

But after a while I got too confident. I jerked the levers too fast to try to make the Clockwork Queen move quicker.

"Slow and steady," Mr Kon warned.

But inside the secret compartment I ignored his words floating through the wood. I was having too much fun controlling the Queen like a wild puppet to slow down.

Then I lost control and jerked one of the levers too far.

The Clockwork Queen's arm thrashed across the board, knocking over the remaining pieces. I heard the *CRASH* and glimpsed the board and its contents tumble to the floor. I tipped the

Queen's head up, and through the periscope I saw Olga laughing silently. Mr Kon did not find it funny.

"Start again," he snapped, hitting an angry fist on the cabinet.

Olga bent down and picked up the fallen chess pieces and board. Then she reset the game.

When she was done, I made the Clockwork Queen repeat her first move.

*

Night had turned to day by the time Olga and I had finished that new game. I went to my lodgings for a nap and returned that afternoon to practise puppeteering the Clockwork Queen some more.

That second day, Olga and I practised late into the night again.

I had been playing as the Clockwork Queen for many hours by then. I'd controlled her through all kinds of different move sequences.

At last Mr Kon announced that I had practised enough. And, anyway, time was up. Tomorrow we would have to leave for St Petersburg to make it to the Winter Palace in time to play the scheduled match against the Empress.

I had plans of my own while I was there. After the game, I had to find some way to talk to the Empress. I would explain to her that I was Ivan Peshka's daughter and beg her to set Papa free. When she heard that I was now alone in the world, she was sure to take pity on us.

8

JOURNEY TO ST PETERSBURG

The journey from the centre of Moscow to the Winter Palace in St Petersburg took almost a week. We travelled on a pair of sledges pulled by horses along frozen snowy roads. The first sledge was attached to the horses, and the second sledge was attached to the first. Mr Kon drove the horses himself.

The first sledge had a cabin where Olga and I huddled together beneath blankets and furs. To pass the time on the journey, I read from Papa's chess book and practised my moves with Olga.

When we weren't playing a game, Olga taught me trick moves that the Clockwork Queen sometimes performed to entertain audiences. Moves like the Knight's Tour, where you made a single knight jump around the board so that it landed on every square once.

The Clockwork Queen travelled on the second sledge along with her cabinet. They were strapped down to stop them shifting around on the journey and covered with a heavy tarpaulin to guard against the snow.

Every evening we would stop and spend the night at a different inn. As soon as we arrived at each place, the innkeeper and Mr Kon brought the Clockwork Queen into the stables along with the horses.

There, Olga and I unstrapped and uncovered the Clockwork Queen, and I climbed into the secret cabinet. I practised puppeteering her until it was time to go into the inn for dinner and bed.

Every night I settled down in my bed and read Papa's chess book, trying to memorise strategies I might use against the Empress.

I wondered what the Winter Palace would be like. Would I get a chance to ask the Empress to release Papa, and if not, how could I use my skill and knowledge to rescue him? How would the Kons help me find Papa? And would they even want to help once we got inside? These thoughts and schemes wavered before my eyes like complex sequences of chess moves each night as I fell asleep.

*

After six days on the road, working the Clockwork Queen had become second nature to me.

On the evening of the seventh day, our sledges arrived at the edge of St Petersburg.

Snowy rooftops glistened in the winter sun. Rows of chimneys puffed smoke into the sky. Boats with white sails drifted along the Neva River, through the city's centre.

Our two sledges clattered along the icy streets towards the Winter Palace, where Papa was imprisoned in the dungeons.

The palace building was so big you could see it from miles away. It dwarfed the houses around it. Its many windows glinted in the last light of the setting sun. The palace's surface was like a massive iced cake covered in gold decorations.

Had Papa been as awestruck as me when he first saw it? I wondered.

The silver gates of the Winter Palace opened with a *CLANG*!

The horses pulled our two sledges into the snowy courtyard and stopped outside a grand entrance.

Mr Kon jumped down from the driver's seat to open the door of our carriage.

"We will have very little time to set up," he whispered to Olga and me as we stepped down from the carriage. "You must pretend to be a servant, Sophie. Make yourself as inconspicuous as possible so no one notices you. Then, when no one's looking, you must sneak off and hide in the Queen's secret compartment."

I took note of what Mr Kon said and tried to melt into the background.

Twelve footmen arrived, followed by a tall stern-looking man with a red nose. The stern-looking man introduced himself as the Empress's personal secretary, Mr Ladya. He was the man who had written me and Mama that horrible letter informing us of Papa's fate.

"You're very late," Mr Ladya said. "But at least you have arrived on the date we agreed. That is something." He clicked his fingers at the footmen, saying, "This way, please."

The twelve footmen untied the Clockwork Queen and carefully carried her and her cabinet into the Winter Palace. Mr Kon and Olga and I followed behind with Mr Ladya.

We followed Mr Ladya and the twelve footmen carrying the Clockwork Queen up a grand marble staircase and along a gold-painted hallway.

I stared open-mouthed at the incredible beauty of everything. Rich tapestries and paintings covered every wall, and the floor was chequered in black-and-white marble, like a chess board.

"The Empress is at dinner," Mr Ladya explained. "She likes a game afterwards. She has commanded that the chess match take place in the small ballroom as soon as possible after your arrival."

We stepped into a magnificent ballroom. Golden chandeliers flickered with hundreds of brightly burning candles. The walls were covered in silks, and the ceiling was painted with images of angels and cherubs on great white clouds. The twelve footmen put down the Clockwork Queen in the centre of the floor and left.

"You must set up as fast as possible," Mr Ladya said. "I will return with the Empress as soon as she has finished her dinner." With that he left too.

Now we were alone, Mr Kon turned to me. "Get into the secret compartment, Sophie," he said. "There won't be another chance before the game."

I nodded, pushing my fear down in my stomach. My first public performance playing as the Clockwork Queen would be against the Empress.

Olga helped me crawl into the secret compartment. She lit a candle and handed it to me, then closed the hidden panel behind me.

It was in the nick of time. Seconds later there was the fanfare of trumpets outside the door. Mr Kon, who was busy setting up the board, was so shocked that he forgot to throw the blanket over the Clockwork Queen, so I could see everything through her eyes as it happened.

I peered through the periscope and watched as the doors to the ballroom flew open and the Empress arrived, followed by a long line of ladies-in-waiting.

9

THE EMPRESS'S SURPRISE

I stared through the periscope at the Empress and her ladies-in-waiting. I tried to keep as still as possible so no one would hear me.

The Empress wore a magnificent black silk dress. Her dark hair was folded into ringlets on each side of her snooty face and braided into two long plaits at the back.

The dresses of her ladies-in-waiting were covered in jewels and embroidery. Their skirts were so large they looked as wide as the length of a horse.

A young boy who was about the same age as me followed them. *This must be Prince Paul*, I thought. The big gold buckles on his shoes jangled as he dragged his feet, clearly bored.

"Is this the Clockwork Queen who plays chess?" asked the Empress.

"Yes, Your Majesty," said Olga with a curtsey.

"I am the creator of the Clockwork Queen," said Mr Kon, bowing deeply. "This is my daughter, Olga. We brought the Queen from Moscow on your command."

"Why, she looks like me!" the Empress exclaimed. Beaming, she peered at the Clockwork Queen, getting so close that I could see every pore on her face through the periscope.

"I hope she is as good at chess as we have been led to believe," the Empress said.

Hidden inside the machine, I felt a bubble of fear burst in my chest.

I was about to take on Catherine the Great, the Empress of Russia. This was a woman who valued chess so much she had called Papa to the palace to teach her son to play. Then she had imprisoned Papa when he had failed to interest Paul in the game. And that had turned my whole world upside down.

I shifted anxiously inside the box, preparing myself at the controls of the Clockwork Queen. Mr Kon and Olga began laying out the pieces on the chess board on the cabinet in front.

Instead of the usual pieces, I had asked Olga to use Papa's pieces from my box. I thought they would bring me luck.

One of the ladies-in-waiting fetched a chair for the Empress.

"Your Majesties," said Mr Kon, turning the key on the side of the cabinet. "I shall now wind the Clockwork Queen."

When he had finished, Mr Kon started the rest of his patter, just as he had last time before the game.

"These are the wheels and gears that move the Clockwork Queen—"

He was cut off by the Empress. "Please," she said. "I cannot bear theatrics. Can we just start the match?"

"As you wish, Your Majesty," Mr Kon said. He closed the cabinet and wound the key on its side one more time for effect.

It made a loud crunching of gears around me, which was my signal to start moving the Clockwork Queen. Using the middle lever, I turned the Queen's head slowly to look around. I made the Clockwork Queen give a nod to the

Empress and the Prince. Then I lowered her gaze to examine the board.

"The game will last an hour, Your Majesties," Olga explained to the royal audience. "The Queen always begins. We allow her the first move out of courtesy as she is made of clockwork."

"No," said Catherine the Great. "I am the Empress. I make the first move."

She turned the board around so that the white pieces were in front of her and moved her queen's pawn to begin play.

Inside the cabinet, I could make out the Empress and the board through the periscope. I gripped the lever to my right and adjusted the various brakes and knobs attached to it. I made the Clockwork Queen pick up my own queen's pawn and pressed it into play. That was my first move.

Almost from the start, my moves forced the Empress to be defensive. After an hour of pulling levers and turning dials to control the Clockwork Queen, I was able to force her into checkmate. I made the Clockwork Queen give three short nods.

The Empress tipped her king and sat back angrily in her seat. She had lost.

I let go of the controls of the Clockwork Queen so that she stilled.

The Empress folded her arms and stared at the machine for a long time. Then she said, "Someone else should play against her. Call Mr Peshka. He should be able to beat this machine. Where is he?"

My heart leapt as I crouched in the secret compartment inside the Clockwork Queen. She was talking about Papa.

"You imprisoned Mr Peshka – remember, Mama?" Prince Paul said. "Because he did not properly teach me the game."

"That's right," the Empress replied, then turned to one of her ladies-in-waiting. "Have Mr Peshka fetched from the dungeons immediately. He will defeat this machine on our behalf."

The call went out down the hall. And everyone waited.

Hidden inside the secret compartment, I held my breath nervously.

I was about to see Papa again. For the first time in two years.

But I would be hidden. He wouldn't know it was me.

At last Mr Ladya arrived, leading a man in rags with a grey beard and long, tangled hair into the room. Could this really be Papa? He looked so different, I barely recognised him. No longer neat and dazzling, but dusty, grey and worn down.

"Mr Peshka," said the Empress as the man was brought before her.

Joy flooded my bones. It *was* Papa.

I watched through the periscope as he looked around the room at everyone. Papa's eyes widened as he took in the Clockwork Queen, Olga and Mr Kon.

"You must be the famous chess master, Ivan Peshka," Mr Kon said.

"That's right," Papa replied. "Pleased to meet you."

He said nothing more. Papa did not reveal to the Empress that he knew the Kons from his old life in Moscow.

"I command you to play against this machine!" the Empress told Papa.

"As you wish, Your Majesty," Papa replied.

Papa sat down in the chair opposite the Clockwork Queen. The Empress took a seat at his right side. The Prince stood to his left. The ladies-in-waiting and Mr Ladya gathered behind them to watch the game.

Papa looked down at the board, and his eyes widened again. He recognised his carved chess pieces. The ones we had always played with in the park when he was teaching me the game. The ones he had given me in the coach station the day he'd left for St Petersburg.

Papa stared carefully into the Clockwork Queen's eyes, and I saw something inside him click. I realised he suspected I was hidden inside the machine.

We were only a short distance from each other, Papa and I. Playing chess. Just as we always used to. Just as we had been when he'd last said goodbye. But this time was under very different circumstances. I was hidden in a cabinet. He was a prisoner of the Empress.

In my hiding place, I grasped the lever to my right and made my first move for the Clockwork Queen.

10

A STRANGE REUNION

The first move I made was the first move Papa
had ever shown me. The King's Pawn Opening.
I was hoping he would recognise it.

Every professional chess player has their
own individual style of play. Papa did too.

I was going to play Papa's style. That way
I could alert him to what he already suspected.
That it was me, Sophie, hidden inside the
Clockwork Queen.

Papa moved his king's pawn in return.

I picked up my king's knight and put it into play, controlling the arms of the Clockwork Queen from inside the box. The game was underway.

*

Papa's play was slow and considered, just like the Clockwork Queen. I had to focus not just on the game but on controlling the Queen's hands to move the pieces.

But still, I was determined to beat him this time.

Papa seemed very interested in the Clockwork Queen. He asked for some paper and a pen and ink so he could write down her moves.

There was a discussion with the Empress, who finally agreed.

As the game went on, I remembered what Papa had said to me the last time we

played: *Practise with my pieces. Learn from the masters. Then, the next time we meet, you will be good enough to defeat me.* I knew now I was good enough.

*

At the end of the game, I cornered Papa's king with my bishop and my queen. Soon it was checkmate.

The Clockwork Queen gave three short nods. She had won again.

I had beaten Papa for the first time in my life. Now I had to find a way to get out of the Clockwork Queen unnoticed and beg the Empress to free him.

But the Empress did not look happy.

"How disappointing, Mr Peshka," the Empress said as she stood from her seat. "You failed to teach my son chess, and you have failed to beat this Clockwork Queen. If you had, I might have reconsidered your sentence. But you lost, so you will remain in prison."

I felt awful. Papa would stay a prisoner because of me. Perhaps he still had a chance if I told the Empress our story?

"Get this Clockwork Queen out of here!" the Empress snapped. "And take Mr Peshka back to his cell! I am sick of chess and grandmasters!"

"As you wish, Your Highness," said Mr Ladya.

"Good," said the Empress. "I never want to see any of them again." She stared menacingly at Papa.

I knew then that she would never release him. I would need to come up with a different plan to get him out.

Mr Kon and Olga looked disappointed. I felt distraught. We had only been in the Winter Palace for a few hours. How would I rescue Papa if we were sent away?

I glanced at Papa one last time through the periscope. I saw him secretly tear off a piece of his paper and slip it under the chess board. I needed that note.

Papa nodded ever so slightly to Mr Kon and Olga. Then he was taken away, followed by the Empress and her ladies-in-waiting, and finally the prince.

When everyone was gone, I saw Mr Kon turn to Mr Ladya.

"My daughter and I can't possibly leave tonight," Mr Kon begged. "It is late and we have nowhere else to go. You promised us lodgings at the palace."

"All right," said Mr Ladya. "You can stay one night. But you must leave in the morning as Her Majesty commanded."

Inside the machine, I let out a sigh of relief. We were staying. If I kept myself hidden inside the Clockwork Queen, no one would know where I was and I might still get the chance to save Papa.

"I shall take you to your sleeping quarters," Mr Ladya told Mr Kon and Olga. "You will be woken at five to pack up your machine and remove it from the palace."

"Thank you," Mr Kon said. He glanced down at the note hidden beneath the chess board. He hadn't had a chance to read it. Instead, he nodded to me inside the machine to indicate that I should take the note.

Mr Kon and Olga followed Mr Ladya out of the room. As they left, Olga sneaked a look back into the eyes of the Clockwork Queen. "Good luck," she mouthed.

I knew then that they'd given me as much help as they could. Rescuing Papa would be up to me, and I would only have tonight to do it.

*

At last I was alone in the ballroom. I climbed from the secret compartment as fast as I could.

Then I snatched Papa's note from beneath the chess board and read it.

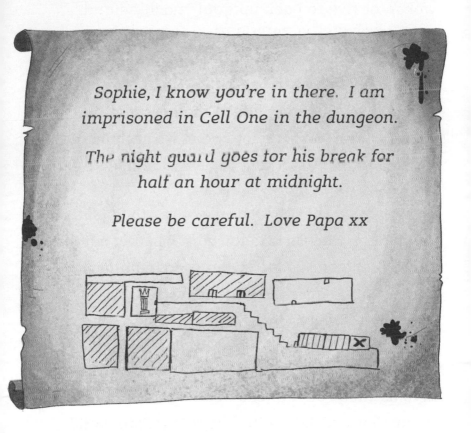

Sophie, I know you're in there. I am imprisoned in Cell One in the dungeon.

The night guard goes for his break for half an hour at midnight.

Please be careful. Love Papa xx

Underneath his words, Papa had drawn a map of the palace. At one end was a drawing of the small ballroom with a chess queen symbol inside to indicate the Clockwork Queen. At the other end, down some stairs, was the palace dungeon and an X for where Papa was being kept.

A clock on the mantlepiece chimed ten. With the note in my hand, I crawled back into the hidden compartment of the Clockwork Queen. I would wait until quarter to midnight, when everyone would hopefully be asleep. I thought nervously about the dangers that lay ahead.

I guessed that fifteen minutes would give me enough time to cross the palace and arrive at the dungeon. Then it would be midnight and Papa's guard would have gone for his break. At least, that's what I hoped.

When I found Papa, I would bring him back here and hide him in the secret compartment of the Clockwork Queen. Then the Kons and I would smuggle him out when we left the palace.

It was the only plan I had. I prayed that we would not be caught. In the meantime, I studied Papa's map and instructions by candlelight.

11

A PAWN IN THE PALACE

The clock on the mantlepiece chimed quarter to midnight. I climbed out of the secret compartment in the cabinet of the Clockwork Queen and crept across the empty ballroom. I clutched Papa's map in my hand. This would be my one chance to rescue him. I had better hurry.

I prised open the door to the ballroom and peered out.

It was dark in the passageway. The chandeliers had been put out. But I was used to darkness. It didn't scare me after the many hours I'd spent hidden inside the secret compartment of the Clockwork Queen.

I sneaked silently along the corridor. I felt like a pawn in a real-life chess game, creeping

across the board. If I could avoid dangers and get to the far side, I could claim my prize – rescuing Papa.

Just as I was thinking this, moonlight poured into the large windows through gaps in the clouds. I saw again the chequered floor, just like a chess board.

I followed the dotted line Papa had marked on his map, passing a corridor full of shining knights' armour and another containing a stuffed horse.

Eventually, I found the stairs down to the dungeon.

I was about to descend when a clock in the passage chimed twelve. I froze, hearing footsteps on the stairs. A hand holding a light suddenly appeared round the corner.

I pulled back from the top step and quickly looked around for somewhere to hide.

To my left was a large model of a castle. I scooted behind it and peered out.

I was just in time. The night guard was at the top of the steps carrying his lantern in one hand and a bag of food in the other. He hadn't heard me, for he walked along casually with not a care in the world. I realised he was leaving for his break, just as Papa had said.

I watched his lantern fading into the distance and cursed myself for almost being caught. Then, when he disappeared, I hurried down to the dungeon.

There were no windows down there, but a faint sliver of light from the stairwell lit up a flagstone floor and a wall of barred doors.

Papa had placed an X by Cell One on the map.

I crept over to it and peered through the barred window.

There he was. Lying on a wooden bed in the corner of a bare room.

Papa opened his eyes at once. He was not asleep, and he had felt me looking at him.

"Sophie!" he cried, beaming. "You got my message. I was sure it was you hidden inside that wicked chess machine. You played all of my old moves! The sequences from my book! Hurry! We have only a half hour until the guard returns."

"Papa," I said, looking around nervously. "Don't talk so loud. Where are the keys?"

"There!" Papa pointed to an alcove further down the corridor.

I felt my way slowly along the wall with an open hand. Luckily my senses had been heightened by many hours in the dark inside the Clockwork Queen. I felt for the keys, grabbed them and returned quickly to unlock Papa's cell.

There was a big bundle of rags further down the hallway. Papa grabbed them and stuffed them into his bed, making a shape that looked exactly like him. Then he drew his blanket carefully over it. If anyone glanced in, they would think he was sleeping.

We locked the cell door and hung the key back on its hook so no one would know it had been used. Then Papa and I snuck off down the passage.

"How will we escape the palace?" Papa whispered as we quietly climbed the stairs. "There are guards at every gate."

"I have a plan," I answered softly. "You just have to be brave, Papa. You can manage that, can't you? *You may not be mighty, but you have courage.*"

Papa smiled to hear his own words from long ago echoed back at him.

"Of course, Sophie," he replied.

We crept carefully back towards the small ballroom and the Clockwork Queen. We stopped at each corner to peer down the next passageway. A couple of times we glimpsed the light of a nightwatchman in the far distance, but no one was ever close enough to see us.

We reached the small ballroom, and Papa shut the door silently behind us. I knelt down by the Queen's feet and pressed the special knot of wood on the rear of the cabinet.

With a *WHOOSH!* the hidden panel slid open to reveal the secret compartment.

"You can hide in here," I said.

"Aha!" Papa smiled. "The pawn becomes the queen! Now I understand!"

I nodded. "Tomorrow we will leave the palace with Olga and Mr Kon and the Clockwork Queen. When we are far enough away, I will let you out. We have to hope we get away before the guard notices you are missing."

Papa was not a tall man, but it was still a squeeze for him to fit into the secret compartment beneath the Clockwork Queen. It was really only designed for a child after all.

With some trouble, he managed it. He couldn't move around, but that was fine. Papa didn't need to puppeteer the Queen. He just had to stay still and hidden.

I kissed his head and shut the secret door on him.

Then I curled up in the dark beneath a corner of the blanket and waited nervously for morning to come.

12

ENDGAME

At first light the following morning, Mr Kon and Olga hurried into the room and saw me.

"Did you do it?" Mr Kon asked softly. "Rescue him?"

I nodded and tipped my head towards the cabinet beneath the Clockwork Queen.

"Oh, thank heavens!" Olga whispered.

Before we could say more, Mr Ladya burst in looking stressed. "We need to move this cabinet right away. The Empress can't find it still here when she wakes."

Mr Ladya took a bell from his pocket and rang it.

Just as they had the day before, the twelve footmen arrived to carry the Clockwork Queen and her cabinet out again. As they were about to pick her up, Papa let out a terrible sneeze from inside the cabinet.

My heart shook. If anyone found out Papa was hidden in the Clockwork Queen, we would all be thrown in the dungeon with him.

Luckily, Olga was standing right beside the cabinet. Thinking quickly, she whipped out her handkerchief and sneezed again just as loudly as Papa. "Excuse me," she said. "I think staying in this draughty palace has given me a cold."

It worked. Everyone thought the first sneeze was her.

Mr Ladya and the footmen turned back to their task. "Hurry up," Mr Ladya grumbled as the twelve footmen picked up the Clockwork Queen.

"She feels much heavier today," one of the footmen complained.

Olga and Mr Kon looked nervously to me to come up with some excuse for this, but I could think of nothing. Thankfully, Mr Ladya was too frazzled to pay attention to him.

The footmen carried the Clockwork Queen and her cabinet down the grand marble staircase and out into the courtyard in front of the palace. The two sledges we had arrived on were waiting for us.

Mr Kon supervised as the footmen strapped the Clockwork Queen and her cabinet in place on the second sledge. Papa sneezed again inside the cabinet, but Olga and I coughed loudly to cover it. Luckily, Mr Kon was already securing the tarpaulin over the Queen and it muffled the sound.

Soon we were ready to depart. Olga and I bundled ourselves into the compartment on the first sledge, and Mr Kon climbed up into the driver's seat.

"I wish you safe travels back to Moscow," Mr Ladya said. "I hope there are no bandits or troubles on the road."

And with that we were on our way.

I held my breath as we reached the gates to the palace.

I was sure someone was going to stop us, search the Clockwork Queen and her cabinet and find Papa hidden in the secret compartment. Then we would all be sent to the dungeons. Surely they must have noticed Papa was missing by now?

But they let us pass.

We flew through the gates into the streets of St Petersburg, then sped onwards to freedom.

*

A light snow was falling by the time we reached the edge of the city.

"That's far enough," Mr Kon shouted from the driver's seat. He pulled on the reins to bring the horses to a stop. "Young lady," he called down to me when the sledge had come to a standstill. "You should go and free your papa at once!"

Olga smiled at me. "Hurry, Sophie," she said. "Your father's probably feeling quite cramped stuck inside the Clockwork Queen for all these hours!"

Quickly, I jumped down from our compartment and ran back to the second sledge where the Clockwork Queen and her cabinet were stowed.

I untied the binding ropes and threw back the tarpaulin. Then I knelt down and pressed the knot of wood to open the secret compartment.

With a *WHOOSH!* the hidden panel slid aside.

Behind it was Papa.

He blinked his eyes in amazement as he saw the bright, cloud-filled sky and the snowy landscape behind me. Then he smiled.

"You did it, Sophie!" Papa cheered as he climbed from that tiny square of darkness and stretched his limbs. He twirled around, taking in the view. "You rescued me!"

Papa hugged me, and I hugged him back.

"*We* did it," I said. "It wasn't me alone. I had some help from your map and our old friends the Kons."

"Of course!" Papa said. "Let's go and thank them."

He took my hand in his. Together we walked away from the Clockwork Queen, up to the front sledge where Mr Kon and Olga were waiting to drive us back to Moscow.

AUTHOR'S NOTE

The story of the Clockwork Queen is based on the real-life history of a machine called the Mechanical Turk. The Mechanical Turk was a clockwork chess player created in the eighteenth century by a man named Wolfgang von Kempelen.

There were many stories about Wolfgang, his wife and their children travelling around Europe demonstrating the Turk to kings, queens and nobles.

One tale that turned out not to be true was that the Mechanical Turk played against the Empress of Russia, Catherine the Great, but the idea of such a contest inspired this story.

Many people believed the Mechanical Turk could really play chess. They imagined it was a complex mechanical robot. But really it was a trick. A human player was hidden in a secret compartment inside the cabinet.

Wolfgang would first show the machine's mechanical workings to the audience. Then the hidden player would get into position in the cabinet to control the Mechanical Turk. They would set up their own reference board inside the compartment to help them play. During the game, they would puppeteer the Turk, making its arms and hands move to take their opponent's pieces.

A few experts realised the Mechanical Turk was a trick. But they didn't know who was controlling it. The cabinet didn't seem big enough to hide an adult. They guessed maybe a child was puppeteering the machine.

Some people suggested that one of Wolfgang's children might be hiding in the cabinet, controlling the machine. But that was never proved.

The Mechanical Turk had many different owners until, eventually, people lost interest in it. Finally, it was broken apart so its secrets would never be uncovered.

After it had been destroyed, a great many chess masters came forward and admitted they had worked the machine. They said it had been interesting playing for the Mechanical Turk, but no one had lasted long in the job because it was so uncomfortable to be hidden in the secret compartment of the cabinet for hours.

*

Catherine the Great was Russia's longest reigning female monarch. After overthrowing her husband Peter III in 1762, she expanded and modernised Russia. She died in 1796 and was succeeded on the throne by her son Paul I.